WAY STATION

WAY STATION

MARY ELIZABETH COUNSELMAN

Rain whipped at the little car, plastering sheets of water against the windshield faster than the wipers could fan it clear. The man at the wheel, crouched forward to peer through the blinding storm, ran a palm quickly over the misted glass; then smiled and patted the knee of the girl pressed close to his side.

"Honey—we can't go on in this downpour. Better pull off the highway, at least until I can see three feet ahead! . . . Cold?" he inquired tenderly, as the slender body shivered against him.

The girl shook her head. "Just . . . nervous, I guess." She smiled back, with a studied attempt at gaiety. "After all, this is my first honeymoon!"

"Some honeymoon!" The bridegroom, a tall stocky young man, whose army uniform contrasted grimly with his bride's frilly suit and flower-hat—laughed wryly. "For so long I've been dreaming of this, slogging around in the rain in Korea . . . A furlough! Ah-h! We'd spend a wonderful, sunny week together in a musical-comedy setting! And what do I get?" He chuckled. "More rain! Besides," he added sheepishly, "I think I took a wrong turn back there someplace. Can't see any road-signs in all this . . ."

He broke off, slowing the car at sight of a byroad at right angles to the paved highway ahead. Pulling off into it, he discovered it to be the entrance of a gravel driveway, ill kept and deeply pitted with holes. As the car jolted to a standstill, deluged by a fresh downpour, a huge truck rumbled past—dangerously close as it hugged the edge of the pavement. The young soldier whistled; tipped back his cap; mopped his face.

"Whew! That was *close!* Can't tell when those trailers will sideswipe you on a wet road . . ."

"Like a dinosaur's tail?" His bride giggled, snuggling against him. "I wasn't worried, Tom. Not with you driving."

The boy grinned, and held her close for a moment. "No? I'm glad you have such confidence in me. Wish *I* had as much! And knew where the merry hell we are!

He rolled down a window glass. Rain lashed at him as he peered out, straining his eyes through the storm-hastened twilight. With a movable search-lamp he swept a yellow arc of brilliance, like a finger pushing at the curtain of rain. It halted abruptly.

"Hey! Some kind of sign up there on a post . . . *FARADAY HOUSE*," he read with difficulty. "*Miss Adelaide Faraday, Prop. Overnight . . .*" A grin curved his anxious mouth. "Well! How about that for luck? It's a tourist home!" The finger of light probed deeper into the rain, seeking out a dim white blur at the end of the gravel drive. "Doesn't look too bad. One of those old Gone-with-the-wind jobs. White-columned veranda, fanlight over the door. They probably serve wonderful meals; fried chicken and biscuits. How about it, Jean baby? Take a look . . ."

The girl was looking—not at the storm-blurred house, but at her husband's earnest expression.

"Anyplace," she whispered. "Any place at all, darling. So long as we can be together, even for . . . a little while." Her eyes misted over suddenly, like the rainy windshield, traveling from the boy's eager young face to the chevrons on his khaki sleeve. "A week! Just a *week* . . ."

The shadow of fear rose between them abruptly at her words, the dark fear of all lovers—that of being separated, of being torn apart by forces stronger than the love that bound them together. The boy reached out, snatched his young bride into his embrace, and held her tight. She clung to him, sobbing.

"Oh, Tommy! If only you didn't have to go back! So . . . so *soon!*"

"Hey, now! We promised to pretend. Remember?" His voice as he tried to comfort her was unsteady, but determinedly light. "Time is relative," he chanted the familiar ritual. "A day can be 24 hours—or a minute. Or *ten years!* We have seven days, hull? Seven times ten are seventy. . . . Why, we've already been married—let's see—fifteen years! Wednesday will be our Golden

Anniversary! And by Friday, when I have to . . . to . . . say, how long can a guy *stand* being married to one old hag?"

The sobbing against his shoulder ceased. With a forlorn but game little sniff, the bride sat up and managed a wavery grin.

"Okay . . ." As the rain slacked briefly, she peered out, following the pointing finger of the searchlight. "It . . . it looks kind of . . . old and rundown. Maybe they won't charge as much as a motel," she added practically, "and we can have more to spend in Florida!"

"Women!" The bridegroom hooted, steering the car up the driveway. "Right in the middle of a tender love-scene, they start worrying about the budget! Can't you dames . . . ever . . . ?"

His voice trailed as the car, following the curve of the gravel drive, came to a halt in front of the big white house they had dimly glimpsed through the rain. On closer inspection, it was very badly in need of repair. Paint curled on the heavy fluted columns, one of which slanted at a dangerous angle. The fanlight over the door looked like a grinning mouth with several teeth out, and the ornate brass knocker was tarnished black; so black that the young couple could barely make out the name engraved on it: FARADAY. Somewhere a shutter creaked on a rusty hinge, with a sound like a groan of pain. Yet, in front of the door, a shabby *Welcome* mat gave a contrasting note of hospitality.

Drenched, shivering, the newlyweds hesitated on the wide veranda. They looked at each other, debating whether to knock or climb back into their car and drive on.

Their decision was made for them, quite without warning, the front door swung open, and a giant Negro in the worn livery of a butler towered over them. His short-cropped kinky hair was snow-white—as were the irises of his eyes, which remained fixed on a point just above Tom's prickling scalp. Involuntarily, Jean gasped and edged closer to her husband, staring up at the man—who was almost seven feet tall. At her slight noise, the milky eyes followed her; and they realized that he was blind.

"We . . . we wondered if . . .? I mean, we saw your sign. And it was raining so hard . . ." Tom's hearty voice gave out.

For the sound of his vibrant young baritone seemed to startle the giant Negro. His eyes, like white agates with their film of cataracts, widened. His lips trembled, then pressed together firmly, as with an effort of self-control.

"*S-sometime I kin hear 'em. . . I kin hear 'em real plain!*" he mumbled, obviously talking to himself. Then, with a sweeping bow reminiscent of a more gracious era when the old mansion was new, he stood aside and gestured them into the hall. "Come in, Suh! And . . . and Ma'm; Faraday House makes you welcome! Miss Addie seen you th'ough a window o' de parlor, and say: 'Saul, you go open de door for our guests! Hit ain't a fit night for *ducks* to be out in!' Miss Addie say . . ."

Prattling on in a high childlike voice, the huge Negro ushered them through the door, bowing and scraping. With apprehensive lifts of the eyebrows, the newlyweds took off their wet coats and hung them on an ornate deer-horn hat rack. They followed uncertainly as the butler beckoned them toward a doorway down the long hall that was lighted only by candles in a series of shimmering crystal candelabra.

"Miss Addie right in here, in de parlor!" the tall Negro gestured again, with a bow. "Her and de . . . de other guests . . ."

Tom and Jean, walking very close together, trailed after him, and peered uncertainly through a door indicated by his sweeping black hand. At the threshold, they paused—aware first of a great paneled room; shabby now with its rotting brocades and velvet draperies, but still as beautiful and inviting as in the days when gray-uniformed soldiers and lovely women in crinoline must have laughed and chattered here.

*

A log fire burned in the fireplace, throwing distorted shadows over the room with its exquisite Colonial furniture and antique bric-a-brac. From a chair near the fire, as they entered, a little old lady rose with the quick fluttering motions of a bird, and came to meet them, smiling with a strange mixture of pleasure and regret on her wrinkled face. She wore a black-lace dress with a velvet collar, pinned at the neck by a handsome coral-and-pearl brooch that matched the coral earrings in her pierced ears. Silvery hair was piled up on her head in a quaint style, many years out of fashion, and fastened thus with a pearl-and-coral comb. By her gala attire, also by their sudden awareness of several other people in the room, Tom and Jean were taken aback.

"Oh . . .!" Jean murmured. "I . . . we didn't mean to break in on a . . . a private party!" she apologized. "Perhaps you don't take tourists anymore?"

"Tourists?" The old lady laughed gently at the word, as though she found it secretly amusing. "Oh! Oh, yes, my dear. You and your . . . your husband?" She glanced astutely from the ring on Jean's hand to Tom's uniform, then nodded. "You and your young soldier-husband are quite welcome here. Newlyweds?" She clucked her tongue at Jean's shy nod and Tom's flush. "How sad!" she murmured. "But at least you're together. Sometimes those who stop here alone are so frightened, so bewildered . . . !"

Tom and Jean looked at her blankly. Then Tom grinned, interpreting her queer words in terms of his uniform and the current war.

"Oh! Yeah. . . . And you say we can get a room for the night? Do you serve meals?"

"Anything you like." The old lady called Miss Addie nodded her head kindly. "Anything to make you . . . comfortable, until you're ready to . . . to go on. Would you like to register?" She gestured toward a dog-eared book on the table, beside which lay a quilled pen and an old-fashioned ink bottle quite empty of ink.

"Yes, of course!" Tom stepped briskly to the table, and flipped open the book. Riffling through the pages to find the last one bearing the present date, he frowned slowly . . .

The last page which bore signatures and addresses of registrants was yellow with age—and was dated ten years ago! He started to lift the pen, then laid it down again, puzzled.

If Miss Addie Faraday kept "overnight guests" for a living, Tom thought, she and her rundown tourist-home were not doing much business. Either that, or her guests—even those now moving restlessly around the friendly, firelit room—did not comply with the national law requiring all paying roomers to register. Something very odd was going on here.

"I . . . believe I'll register later," Tom said cautiously, glancing around at the other occupants of the room. "Will that be all right?"

"Quite all right," Miss Addie nodded amiably. "And now . . . Would you like to go straight to your room? I see you have no luggage . . ."

Tom dug into his pocket at once. "It's . . . it's still in the car. But we want to pay in advance, anyway . . ." He fumbled in another pocket, a slow flush creeping over his face. "Gosh! Can't seem to find my . . . my wallet . . .! Could I have dropped it when we . . . we got out of the car?"

Old Miss Faraday's expression of gracious welcome did not change, except for a slight quirk of kindly amusement at the corner of her wrinkled mouth. She held up her hand, speaking calmly, soothingly, as to an upset child.

"Don't trouble yourself about it. You can pay me when you . . . check out. And Saul will take care of your luggage . . . *Saul?*" She raised her sweet, birdlike voice, and the giant Negro reappeared in the doorway. "This gentleman thinks he may have dropped his wallet outside. Will you look for it, please? And their luggage? Of course, there's no hurry . . ."

There was, Tom noted with growing suspicion and annoyance, a definite note of amusement in the old lady's voice, as though she were playing some sort of game—a secret game in which the tall butler shared, somewhat sulkily.

"Yas'm," he bowed. "Anything else, Miss Addie?"

"No . . . no." His mistress fluttered a hand pleasantly. "Not just now. Perhaps later the young people will like a snack served in their room. Honeymoon-style . . . eh?" From somewhere in the folds of her lace gown, she actually produced a little ivory fan, and pretended to tap Tom's wrist with it playfully. "Partridge? Saul shot two or three yesterday, out in the north pasture. His dog, Feather, has been trained to bark when she points. Saul fires at the sound of their wings. Partridge—he's quite lucky with partridge. They *whir*, you know . . ."

"No kidding?" Tom, a demon-hunter himself, could not help a boyish exclamation at her words. "Say, honey, did you hear what . . .?"

He turned to Jean—and broke off as their eyes met. The gracious air of hospitality about this old house, with its tiny silver-haired hostess and its giant black menial, was an insidious force disarming and relaxing him like the fire blazing on the hearth. His eyes traveled swiftly over the other occupants of the room—transients, evidently; a hodgepodge assortment of tourists who were acquainted neither with Miss Addie nor with one another.

His alert gaze singled out one—an elderly man wearing, of all things, a pair of stained overalls and a battered old straw-hat. He was pacing about nervously, a distraught look on his weather-beaten face, when Miss Addie moved to his side with the casual air of a good hostess drifting about among her guests.

"Can I get you something, sir?" she asked in that caroling voice like a songbird's. "Do sit down by the fire and rest yourself. You mustn't fret. Really, there's nothing to worry about . . . *now.*"

The old man, a farmer from his speech and dress, gave her a quick, seemingly desperate look, twisting his gnarled hands together.

"Ma'm—how'd I git here?" he blurted all at once, in a voice edged with hysteria. "I . . . I don't recollect *nothin'* . . .! Except, I went out to put the cow in the barn, h'it was a-rainin' so hard. And then that sharp pain struck me, right here in the chest! I called to Sarah, that's m' sister, she's bedridden . . . And I kinda remember walking along some dark road or other . . . Then, all at once, I'm *here!* . . . Who . . .? Where . . .? I got to git back to Sarah! She can't *do* for herself! She's paralyzed . . . !"

"There, there." Miss Addie's quiet voice edged into his outburst, like a lark's singing in a lull of gunfire. "You mustn't be frightened or worried about your sister. Someone will take care of her. I'll phone the county health officer, if you'll tell me your name and address. . . ."

"Wilkins. I got a little farm," the man blurted out eagerly. "Two mile east of Hopper's Ferry, on Highway 6. There's . . . there's just me and m' sister. But I got a boy in Atlanta! He'd come a-runnin' if he knew his aunt . . . if he knew I . . . No!" He shook his head stubbornly. "No, I got to git back some way! There's the stock, and there's my crop o' cotton. . . ."

"Please." The mistress of Faraday House spoke again, melting his hysteria with gentleness. "You must get hold of yourself. *And . . . you must realize that you can't go back. You can only go . . . on, Mr. Wilkins.*"

Frankly eavesdropping, Tom and Jean stared at each other in blank astonishment. *Why* couldn't this frantic old farmer go back to his work and his bedridden sister? Why was Miss Addie telling him that in such a sad, gentle manner? Her soothing voice was insistent, almost hypnotic. Under its spell, a drowsy peace pervaded the room. Its occupants stopped shifting about. Voices lowered to a calmer pitch. . . .

Jean started. Something like a chill breeze had brushed her bare arm. Looking down, she was aware of a thin, hollow-eyed little girl, about seven years old, staring up at her with an almost terrifying intensity. She was wearing. . . . Jean gasped. Why, the child had on a pink flannel nightgown, and was barefooted! Perhaps she had wandered downstairs, she decided quickly, away from sleeping parents yet unaware that she had slipped out of bed.

The child's lips parted slowly in a vague, wistful smile.

"Are . . . are you my mother?" she whispered unexpectedly. "Daddy said I would . . . would see my Mommy soon! But I don't . . ." The thin mouth quivered. "I don't know what she *looks* like! She went away when I was borned, and . . . and there was only a snapshot Daddy had. Her hair was long and goldy, like yours!" she added, hopefully. "You *do* look kind of like the picture. . . !"

Jean's heart contracted. She reached out to gather the child into her embrace. *Poor little thing*, she thought fiercely. Deserted once by her mother, and now tossed back to her by a father who evidently did not want her either. . . ! Her reaching hands almost touched the thin arms. But shyly, fearfully, the little girl backed away at her words:

"Darling—no. No, I'm not your Mommy . . . But aren't you cold, running around in your little nightgown and bare feet?" Jean smiled and held out a hand coaxingly. "Come let me take you back up to your room. Is your Daddy asleep upstairs? Does he know you've slipped out. . . ?"

The child's dark eyes stared up at her. The pale lips puckered— with disappointment, or bewilderment, or something Jean could not define.

"I . . . don't know where my Daddy is, either!" she whimpered, near tears. "He was at the hospital, right by my bed. And he . . . he was *crying!* And telling me about my Mommy, about how I'd be seeing her soon . . . You're sure you're not my . . .?" she asked again, with pathetic eagerness.

Tom and Jean exchanged a helpless look, torn with pity.

At that instant, Miss Addie drifted over to them, smiling kindly from the child to Jean in a way that puzzled the newlyweds.

"Look over there in that glass case!" the old lady said cheerily to the little girl. "It's just chock- full of china dollies I used to play with, when I was a little girl! That's the one. Yes! . . ." As the child, bemused, moved toward the cabinet across the room, the old lady sighed. "Oh *dear!*" she murmured. "It's always like this with the children.

Unless someone who's gone . . . on ahead comes back for them, to show them the way. Did she mention a mother?" Miss Addie asked hopefully.

"Why . . . why, yes!" Jean and Tom, over the silvery head, exchanged a shocked look. "A mother who deserted her as a baby! Who's supposed to meet her and . . . Look," Jean snapped. "You don't mean that poor little tike has nobody *with* her? She's traveling *alone?*"

"Most of them are." Miss Addie shrugged cryptically. "That's . . . that's why they stop here. Because they can't go back, of course—and they're afraid to go on. You're two of the *lucky* ones!" Her faded blue eyes traveled sadly from Tom to Jean. "You're together, so it isn't as . . . confusing. Oh *mercy!*" She broke off, fluttering her ivory fan in delicate agitation. "Can't you take the child on with you, if no one comes for her? The older ones do that, lots of times. Really, she'd be no trouble."

Jean gaped at her. "*Take* . . .? You're asking *us* to . . . ?"

She broke off, startled, as wind or a sudden freshet of rain clattered a window of the firelit room. Glancing toward the sound, the honeymooners pointed and cried out at sight of a dim face pressed against the panes— a woman's face, framed by long flowing hair the color of Jean's.

At their exclamation, the little girl, peeking forlornly at Miss Addie's doll-collection, turned. An expression of wonder and delight illuminated her thin features at sight of the face outside the window.

"*Mommy! There's* my Mommy . . . ! I'd know her anywhere . . . !"

The words seemed torn from her, a glad cry, trailing after her as she pelted, barefoot, into the hall. The dim face vanished from the window, and Jean and Tom heard the front door open and close. But what amazed them most was the look of beaming complacence on the face of old Miss Faraday, fluttering her dainty fan with a new composure.

"Well," the old lady said in pleased voice, "*that's* settled. And now, if I can only make that poor Mr. Wilkins understand! Saul tells me I *simply can't* afford any more long-distance calls, or I'd just phone that son of his in Atlanta . . . Hmm. There must be *some* way to help . . . !"

Pursing her wrinkled lips, Miss Addie bustled across the room to another guest—a disheveled youth with a nasty-looking bruise on his forehead. The honeymooners glanced at each other sharply as the old lady's clear, birdlike tones drifted to their ears:

"Young man . . .? Are you quite comfortable? Is there anything you'd like? Anyone I can . . . notify?"

The boy, a defiant look on his face, glared up at her from where he sat, hunched on a brocade loveseat. He reached into his sport jacket, mouth quivering, then searched another pocket, muttering under his breath.

"Nah!" he snarled. "How'd I get here? Tell me that! I know when my jalopy blew a tire . . . but after that, I . . . I . . . Who brought me here? What kind of a joint *is* this, anyhow? And how much is it gonna cost me? . . . And where the hell is my pint?" His voice rose, savagely defensive, like that of a wild creature trapped in an animal-pit. "I had almost half a pint left in my . . . !"

Miss Addie sat down beside him serenely, not ruffled in the least by his youthful belligerence.

"Your whiskey?" she said pleasantly. "Perhaps you drank it, son, and . . . and threw the flask away, just before your . . . your accident . . . So *many* of them these days!" She clucked her tongue sadly. "I've had seven this month, would you believe it? Young people, all of them. *So* young, like yourself—with so many good years ahead of you!"

The boy's face twitched. Bleary eyes peered at Miss Addie as through a fog, widening slowly as he seemed to understand more than her casual conversation offered on the surface.

"You . . . you mean I'm . . .?" Tom and Jean heard his hoarse, frightened curse. "That quick, huh?" His defiant mouth twisted wryly, his fingers snapping with a small *pop* that might have been a twig breaking on the hearth. "Just like that, and it's all over?"

Old Miss Faraday smiled. "All over? My *dear!* It's only the *beginning!* 'To sleep; perchance to dream . . .' That was what bothered Hamlet, you know. Because, he wasn't sure it was the end. Just *pouf!* Just . . . oblivion.

Which, of course, it *isn't!*" The ivory fan fluttered, almost flirtatiously, in front of the young man's face. "That's what these poor—well, the ones who do it themselves, believing it's a way out—That's what *they* discover, almost at once! There was one who came here last April, a young girl who had . . . ah, made rather a mess of her life and had decided she couldn't face the music. But, naturally," Miss Addie's cheery laugh rose above the subdued murmur of other voices in the quiet room, "she still had the same problems. Only, she couldn't *get a*t them. She couldn't go back and work them out, poor and . . . and fix things. She had around here, weeping and blaming herself, for weeks! Because there was a very simple solution to her problem, if she'd only sat down and thought it out, instead of . . . But then, of course," the old lady shrugged placidly, "it was too late. She couldn't go back and . . .and fix things. She had to go on, with her life ahead complicated by what she had left undone. . . . Poor child! If she'd only used her . . . her body more constructively, white she had one."

The boy hunched beside her nodded miserably. "Yeah . . . That goes for me, too, huh?"

"That goes for everybody, at some time or another," Miss Addie said gently. "So, it's wicked to complicate . . . living for those we leave behind us to straighten out. You understand?" The youth jerked his head in another helpless nod. "Sure, sure! *Now* you tell me—!" he burst out, bitterly sarcastic.

"Why, I'm pretty sure your parents told you the same thing," old Miss Faraday said, in a mildly chiding manner. "Or your pastor, or some favorite teacher. Or . . . well, if you had any gumption, you'd have just figured it out for yourself!"

The boy grinned sheepishly. "All right! So I knew better! What do I do now? How can I . . .?" His face crumpled again in sudden youthful dismay. "How can I ever make it up to Mom? And . . . and Dad? What can I *do* . . .?"

Old Miss Faraday gave a little shrug, oddly comforting in its finality, despite its gentle reproof.

"You'll have to leave it up to your brothers and sisters, if you have any," she said briskly. "Maybe *they* can make up for . . . the things you say you've done or left undone. As for now," she smiled at the boy, not unkindly, "you must go on. And try to do better at . . . the next place. You realize," she added sternly, "you won't be given the same chances as . . . as, say, that old Mr. Wilkins over there? Poor man, he's done his best. So I'm sure he'll be given wonderful advantages where he's going. If he can only reconcile himself to the fact that he *can't go back!*"

Jean and Tom, still frankly listening in on these double-entendre conversations, nudged each other. Their puzzled eyes drifted to a little group of three oddly-assorted people near the fireplace: a crabbed old man, a leggy bobby-soxer chewing gum, and a wizened little man with slanted eyes who looked as if he might be a Chinese laundryman. As they stared, Miss Addie drifted back to them, following their look with a faint smile.

"The 'flu epidemic," she explained lightly. "They've been comparing symptoms all evening! Ah, well—it gives them something in common," she laughed with a gay flutter of her fan. "*They* won't be lonely on the way, those three, for all they're so different!"

Tom cleared his throat nervously. "Uh . . . I wonder, could we go up to our room now? And have that little snack you promised? Partridge!" He smacked his lips, winking at Jean. "I don't suppose you'd have any wine? A dry wine, like Sauterne?"

"Why, yes," their tiny hostess bobbed her silver head graciously, "I believe there's a bottle or two left, down in the wine cellar. My brother was fond of good wine," she said pleasantly, "though he never drank too much for . . . safety, like that nice boy over there. Such a biddable lad!" Miss Addie glanced back at him, still hunched on the loveseat with his tousled head in his hands. What a pity!"

"He . . . was in some kind of car accident?" Tom asked cautiously.

"Yes." The blue eyes flitted from him to Jean, with a sad look of understanding. "Like you two," and before they could correct her, she hurried on: "Saul will bring up your luggage presently . . . er . . . as soon as he can. Did you see a door just at the head of the staircase? That room will do nicely for you. Just go on up, won't you? I . . . I really must stay down here with these other poor dears. Some of

them are . . . really quite troubled, as I'm sure you've noticed. I must do what I can to . . . to comfort them. May I look in on you later in the evening?" She beamed at them, almost fatuously. "It's such a pleasure to have guests who have . . . well, as Saul says, decided to cooperate with the inevitable!"

"Yes . . . sure! D-drop up to see us later . . ." Tom gulped.

Swapping another bewildered look the honeymooners left the parlor with its queer collection of occupants, and mounted the great curving staircase that swept upward from the hall. Pressed close to his side, Jean whispered:

"What's going *on* here? That weird old lady! Telling everybody they 'can't go back', that they must 'go on'! And that little girl . . . ! Why, she ran out into the rain in her *nightgown*, Tom! And Miss Faraday didn't even try to stop her! And that poor old farmer—*why* can't he go on back to his sister who's bedridden? Did you ever *hear* anything like that old woman . . .?"

"No, I never did!" Her husband laughed shortly. "You know what I think?" he growled. "I think that big Negro picked my pocket as I came in the door! And . . . and they're going to steal our luggage and maybe sell the car. . . . Look, baby," he stopped grimly on the stairway, listening to the faint voices below, "we're getting out of here! We . . . why, I wouldn't spend the night in a creep-joint like this for all the tea in . . . *Oh-oh!*"

His words ended in a curse. At the head of the dim-lighted stairway the giant Negro, Saul, was looming like a dark genie waiting to show them into their room. There was a tray in his great ham-like hand—a tray set for two, with a delicious-looking grilled partridge for each of them, and a wicker-covered bottle of Sauterne. In spite of how his stomach knotted with apprehension, Tom's mouth watered. They had not eaten, he remembered, since breakfast—many hours and miles away from this strange old house just north of the Florida Line.

"Miss Addie say, 'Put dem young honeymooners in de Lavendar Room'!" The tall servant was prattling, again bowing and gesturing them through an open door. "And here de partridge and de wine y'all done ordered, suh. Compliments o' de house!. . . . *All dis-yeah good food*," his childish voice sank to a mumble, "*goin to waste!*

*Cook, cook, cook!" Saul mumbled pettishly. "Don'
nobody but me and Miss Addie eat ary bite o' all dem
victuals! Feather, he goin live high dis week! Us two
cain't eat all dat stuff she tell me to fix for de
guests . . . !"*

Hesitantly, rolling their eyes at each other, Tom and
Jean entered the bedroom, not daring to antagonize that
giant black. Blind he might be—but he could crush them
between those two great hands, wring their necks like
chickens before they could cry out. *If*, Tom thought
helplessly, any of those bizarre people downstairs would
come to their aid . . . !

"Th-thanks," he stammered, as Saul lit a beautiful
hand-painted lamp beside the tester-bed and set his
loaded tray alongside it.

"Er . . . I'd like to tip you, but I . . . I don't seem to
have any change on me . . ." Tom fumbled in his pockets
again, a reflex-action. "You didn't find my wallet outside
in the drive did you? And what about our luggage?"

The agate-eyes of the blind Negro fixed on a point
above his head, polite but sulky—as though Tom should
have known better than to ask such a foolish question, As
no doubt he should have, Tom thought grimly!

"Nawsuh. Ain't see no wallet, ain't had time to tote yo'
luggage. . . . *Wallet! Luggage!"* the childish voice fell to
mumbling again, pettishly. *"Be mighty nice, now, if ive
did git holt o' some change-money! What wid de taxes*

pilin' up, an' us needin' a new well-pump, an' . . . Ma'm?" The white eyes fixed on Jean as she whispered something urgently to Tom about getting out of there, possibly by the back door.

"N-nothing!" Jean quavered. "I . . . I was just saying what a pretty room this is!" she chattered nervously. "This lovely old four-poster bed . . ."

"Yas'm," Saul bobbed politely. "Dis-yeah Miss Addie's room. *Ain't no others cleaned up . . . And I ain't fixin' to do no dustin', and makin' beds nobody don't sleep in!"* the huge Negro was mumbling again. "Miss Addie say, *"Have everthing like it was jest nachel. But I say, ain't no sense in it! Dem guests o' her'n ain't goin' eat nothing', ain't goin' sleep in no bed, and de biggest balance of 'em don't stay no time a-tall . . . ! In and out, in and out . . . !"* The mumble continued irascibly, until at Tom's cough, Saul asked: "Anything else I can do for y'all, suh and ma'm? Miss Addie say, make you comf'able . . ."

"Oh, we're . . . very comfortable!" Tom managed, scanning the big high-ceilinged bedroom for another exit. There was only one, he saw with a sinking heart; and doubtless this ebon giant would station himself outside that door to make sure they did not escape.

"Den I'll bid you a good night, suh and ma'm!" Saul, with another old-world bow, backed through the door, but called back: "Miss Addie say she'll drap up to see y'all in a few minutes, after she 'tend to de other guests."

"Er . . . that's nice!" Jean said brightly, but as the door closed, her face took on an expression of dismay. "Oh, Tom!" she whimpered. "What are they planning? How can we get out of this . . . this . . .? That old lady is as crazy as a loon; you realize that, don't you?"

Her young husband nodded grimly. He tugged at his collar. "Yeah! That's pretty obvious! The thing I *don't* know is, what she has that big ogre of a servant *do* to her 'overnight guests!' Is this one of those murder-for-profit inns you read about . . .? Aw, honey!" his tone changed quickly as Jean's eyes dilated with terror. "I didn't mean to scare you. We'll get out of this . . . somehow!"

His pretty bride sank down on the tester-bed, removing her little flower hat and kicking off her shoes. The feather mattress sank under her invitingly, and she lay back, closing eyes dark-circled with fatigue.

"This is wonderful! I'm so-o tired . . . . It seems we've been driving forever . . ."

Tom was eyeing the tray of partridge and wine. Tentatively he nibbled a piece, then shrugged and opened the wicker- covered bottle.

"If this is poisoned," he said airily, "it's a pleasant way to go! Mm-*mm!*" He smacked his lips over the delicate fowl. "Have some, honey?"

Jean grinned, and held out her hand for a browned wing. "What can we lose?" she pointed out wryly. "Oh, darling, I'm . . . I'm *scared!* What if . . . if they mean to . . . ?"

She stopped speaking, with a gasp as a light knock sounded on the bedroom door.

"It's only I!" Miss Faraday's birdlike carol came through the closed portal. "May I come in?"

"Y-yes! Yes, come in . . . !" Jean called, sitting up with a panicky look at her husband.

They braced themselves as the door swung open, prepared for anything—even the sight of gigantic Saul following his mistress in with an axe in his great hands.

But Miss Addie was alone. She tiptoed in, still winnowing her small fan with coquettish grace, and sat down in a lovely old chair beside the bed. Tom and Jean watched her warily as she beamed up at them, sadness and humor an odd mixture in her expression.

"Well!" she said merrily. "I see you've made yourselves right at home. Saul will bring up your . . . er . . . luggage in a little while," she added in the placating voice of an adult promising a crying child the moon. "In the meanwhile, you just. . . rest. Hm? And . . . ah . . . accustom yourselves to . . . to . . . the realization that, although where you're going will be *different*, it won't necessarily be *worse* than . . . well, what you've just left behind!" she finished, like a diplomat carefully wording an important speech. "Are you beginning to understand? It's only that everyone fears change, and tries to cling to the familiar, the well-known . . ."

Tom did not dare look at his young wife. Elaborately casual, he strolled over to the bedside table again and took another delicious morsel from the tray. Somewhere he had heard that if one would humor a lunatic, and then carefully divert his attention from his obsession. . . .

"Wonderful food . . . !" he murmured, and was opening his mouth for another bite when he noticed Miss Faraday staring at him. Her expression was that of supreme shock, bordering on consternation. She stood up, pointing a shaky finger at him.

"Why, you . . . you're *eating!*" she gasped. "And . . . and drinking!"

Tom lowered the morsel of bird and the tiny wine glass, stiffening. He looked at Jean, who was clutching her throat.

"Yes!" Tom snapped. "Of course I'm eating. Is the food poisoned?"

"No! No, certainly not!" Miss Addie panted, sinking back into her chair as if the shock of what she saw was too much. "It's only that . . . that . . . none of them ever . . . I mean, they only *think* they're hungry. It's just a thought-habit carried over from . . . from . . ."

She was interrupted by a loud hammering on the door. It burst open, and the blind Negro, drenched to the skin, plunged into the room. A damp wallet— Tom's wallet—was clutched in his outthrust black hand.

"Miss Addie!" he burst out in agitation. "Dey's a *car* out yonder in de driveway! I run slap into it a minute ago, when I went out to call Feather in out'n de rain! And . . . and he was totin' somep'm around in his fool mouth, like he always do— a slipper, or anything he pick up." Dark sensitive fingers ran ever the object, seeing what the blind eyes could not. "Feel like a man's wallet! And hit's plumb full o' foldin' money!"

"It's mine," Tom snapped, reaching out and taking it from the trembling black hand almost bruskly. "I *told* you I must have dropped it when we . . ."

"*Saul*—!" Miss Addie was fluttering her fan again, with a visible effort at composure. "Saul," she interrupted, half in dismay, half in amusement, "these two guests aren't like the others. They . . . I realized it when I saw this nice young man eating your partridge."

"*Eatin'!*" The white eyes bulged in the ebon face. "Y-you mean dey ain't . . . ?"

No," Miss Addie began to laugh weakly. "No, Saul, they're just like us." She turned to Jean and Tom then, with a gracious smile of apology. "You poor children! Stumbling out of the storm into a . . . a place like this! I naturally thought you were one of the usual . . . ah . . . travelers who stop here. We haven't had a genuine paying-guest," she confessed gaily, "for over ten years!"

*

The tall Negro grinned feebly, nodding. "Naw'm. Sho' ain't." His face brightened as Tom shoved a damp bill into his hands. He felt it lovingly with a big calloused thumb. "*Money!*" he said with a happy grunt. "Us sho' could *use* some! Them as ain't alive might not need it no mo', Miss Addie. But us two is *still livin'!*"

"From hand to mouth," Miss Addie said cheerfully. "Still . . ." She lifted her silver head proudly, "I haven't had to mortgage Faraday House. We manage. Of course, my hospital bills took all our savings—everything but the place and a few acres. Saul hunts and farms, even raises a little livestock. Now and then I sell off one of the family heirlooms when we're desperate for cash. . . . But, there!" she broke off, engagingly. "I mustn't burden two lovebirds with my silly troubles! I only hope," she smiled apology once more, "that what you've seen here hasn't . . . upset you too much?"

Jean and Tom smiled back at her unsteadily. There was something so disarming about this sprightly old lady. And yet, obviously, she was a mental case! They stiffened once more at her next words; offered in a light conversational tone as if she were talking about the weather.

"You see, they've been coming here—the lost, bewildered ones like those you saw downstairs in the parlor—for eight years. Or is it nine?" she interrupted herself to peer up, bird-wise, at the giant Negro. "How long, Saul? Wasn't it 1945 when that policeman wandered in here, saying he had been shot in a holdup, in Traceyville? Poor thing! He kept trying to call headquarters, to give them a description of the bandit who shot him and wounded that gas-station attendant! As if it mattered to him *then!* Although," Miss Addie laughed, "we didn't realize . . . *what he was.* Not until after Saul took him upstairs. I called a doctor. But when we went up to the room, he was gone! There wasn't even any blood on the bedsheets and pillow, of course. Because . . . *they* have no substance. He only *thought* of himself as bleeding; so that's how I saw him, before he went on."

Over her head, warily, Tom and Jean locked glances. *Crazy!* their eyes exchanged wordlessly. *But, harmless?* When would her lunacy take a dangerous turn . . . ?

"Entirely weightless and without force of any kind," Miss Addie went on brightly. "That business about chain-rattling is ridiculous! They can't move solid objects, any more than a . . . a TV image could! Why, they can't possibly harm anyone or help one, either. That's what bothers them. One minute they can eat, drink, move heavy objects, fight, and so on. Then . . . *pouf!* They're no more than smoke. A thought-form, as I said. What we see is simply a . . . a *picture* of them, as they remember themselves. If they thought of themselves naked," the old lady tittered naughtily, "why, that's how we'd see them! But they think *clothes*, as well as *hair* and *skin* and so on. Even watches and jewelry, sometimes! Anything they feel strongly was a part of their personality in the . . . the material world they have just left. Of course, to *see* them, one must be either psychic . . . or very tired, ill, or feverish—any condition that would let the Sixth Sense come into play."

"Oh! I . . . I see," Jean gulped. "What you're trying to tell us," she stammered lamely, "is that . . . those people downstairs are . . . are all . . . ?"

"Yes," old Miss Faraday inclined her head daintily. "Quite right, my dear. I don't know why they come *here!*" She laughed, with a merry flirt of the little fan. "Unless," she pursed her lips pensively, "it's because I died, and they feel a . . . a sort of kinship . . ."

Jean rolled her eyes at her husband. Tom, sipping his wine, choked.

"You . . . *d-died?*" he coughed. "Then you think you . . . uh . . . I mean, you're like them, too?"

"Oh, no!" Miss Addie emitted a silvery laugh full of innocent merriment. "No, no, I'm very much alive *now*. As alive as you are, you two nice young people! But I did die, about ten years ago—1943, wasn't it, Saul? Medically, you understand. There are degrees of death, as it is accepted by . . . ha, ha! What we call scientific fact."

The fan brushed away Science airily, as if it were an annoying insect. "Some years ago, if breathing stopped, one was considered dead. But then they found a way to use artificial respiration, and make the lungs work again. Before that, consciousness was considered 'life'—and the unconscious were medically 'dead.' Many people in a state of trance were even buried alive, during the early days of medicine. But medicine is making such strides, there may come a day when the soul can be switched from one body to another! Naturally, a body is only a clumsy container for one's real *self* . . ."

Tom ran his finger around under his collar, moving across the room to Jean's side. They sat, very close together, under the canopy of the big bead where General Beauregard, or Robert E. Lee, might very well have slept once. The old lady's matter-of-fact voice, reeling out mad words that, somehow, sounded so amazingly sane, held them spellbound with attention.

"Later in this century," Miss Faraday was saying, "a person was not pronounced 'dead' unless he had no pulse. Stimulants were used to start it up again; but if they failed, that was all. And that," she announced blandly, "was what happened to *me*. My heart stopped beating during an emergency operation to remove my appendix. Right there on that very bed you're sitting on! It was too late to rush me twenty-eight miles to the hospital in Mentonia. So . . . I died. My spirit left my body."

The newlyweds gaped at her. Miss Addie chuckled at their expressions.

"That is," she continued, her faded eyes twinkling, "I was dead for about thirty seconds. The doctor Saul phoned was out, and a young assistant came in his place. It was he who operated . . . and he had once happened to witness a miracle-operation by one of the big surgeons at Johns-Hopkins. A . . . a *tho* . . ."

The old lady wrestled with her failing memory, then came up with the medical term: "A *thoracotomy*. You know? Where the surgeon opens the chest cavity and massages the heart until it starts beating again? This young doctor of mine decided to try it on me. I was dead—so there was nothing to lose, he figured. And it worked!" Miss Addie bowed, fluttering her fan complacently. "I was brought back from the dead. Like Lazarus—poor man!" she added thoughtfully. "I know now why he was so *quiet*, afterward. There's so much I could tell you!" she sighed. "But I can't prove it, so nobody would believe me. Therefore, I've just learned to keep my mouth shut, and let them find out for themselves! Everyone will find out—sooner or later."

The newlyweds pressed closer together, disturbed yet soothed by an air of calm knowledge in their hostess's manner. Rain whispered against the window-panes.

Somewhere a dog howled mournfully, as though to emphasize the old lady's last sentence.

"Dat Feather!" Saul grunted suddenly, jolting them from their dream-like trance. "Hollerin' his haid off 'cause he wet and cold! I'm got to go down and fotch him into de kitchen . . ." Still mumbling, the blind giant lumbered out, groping his way with uncanny accuracy through the old house he had grown up in, and which was his whole world.

Miss Addie glanced after him fondly. She sighed. "My, I don't know how I'd get along without Saul! He's the grandson of a Faraday slave, and I'm willing this place to him when I die. . . . When I *really* die!" she added, with a twinkle of humor in her eyes. "He does put up with a lot from me, Saul does. Especially about my . . . overnight guests! He can't see them, of course, and he claims he can't hear them! Whether it's only because they make so much extra work for him, I don't know," she smiled. "I . . . try to make them feel as natural as possible when they come here," she explained gently. "Poor things— they fight against going, some of them! Most are just . . . bewildered. All they want is . . . well, road-information. Or just a place to pause and think, until they get over the shock of suddenly being dead!"

"Oh! Oh, yes . . . I . . . I can see that," Jean managed a sickly smile. She squeezed Tom's hand, unseen by the old lady, signaling him as she said: "It's . . . been wonderful, stopping by here. And we want to pay for the full night. But . . . we really must go on, now that the storm has slacked up some. Er . . . what we wanted, too, was road-information. Are we far from Eltonville?

I have an aunt there," she lied desperately. "We . . . er . . . we promised to stay overnight with her, and if we don't do it, this near . . . I'm sure you understand?"

Old Miss Faraday's blue eyes searched Jean's face knowingly. She smiled, with a tiny, almost invisible shrug.

"Of course, dear," she said graciously. "Of course I understand. Eltonville is only eight miles on from here. A nice hotel there. Really, a haunted house," her eyes twinkled, "is no place for a honeymoon. Eh?"

"Oh, I . . . I didn't mean . . . !" Jean floundered. "It's only that . . ."

"Yes!" Tom came to her rescue. "This aunt of my wife's—she's expecting us. And if we don't come rolling in sometime tonight, she's liable to think . . . uh . . ."

". . . that you've joined my . . . my 'overnight guests?'" the old lady finished, with a sly wink. "You may have noticed my sign as you drove in," she added, with girlish giggle of mirth. "Did you look at it closely? You know, I sometimes wonder if *it* isn't the reason they use Faraday House as a . . . a sort of way station, I call it. I wonder if there are other way stations, like this one? Places where they . . . ? If I were sure it *wasn't* what brings them here,

I'd take it down—that sign." She smiled. "We really don't take overnight guests anymore. At least, not the kind who expect A-1 accommodations! I'm too old . . . and it makes too much work for Saul, cleaning and carrying luggage and the like. Besides," Miss Addie said complacently, "I manage to get along without money, in this little halfway house of mine!

Halfway between life and death, one might say. . . . Oh! You leaving now? I'll see you to the door. . . "

Steering down the winding gravel drive a few moments later, Tom and Jean looked back through the rain at the big white-columned house. They had left, they realized, in rather an abrupt hurry—without even a glance into that peaceful, firelit parlor, where had been assembled such an unusual assortment of people. Bidding Miss Addie good-bye hastily, they had dashed out to the little car standing in the rain—almost tripping over a friendly-looking Irish setter, which trotted back into the house at a whistle from the butler. The great front door had not even closed before Tom started the motor and took off in second-gear.

But now, at the end of the driveway, Tom braked the car, strangely loathe to lose sight of that hospitable old mansion, with its quaint bird-like hostess and childlike black genie of a servant. They turned, looking back for a long thoughtful moment. Then Tom laughed shortly, patting his young bride on the knee.

"Of course you know," he chuckled, "those . . . *guests* weren't there at all. We've been victims of mass-hypnosis. What with that old lady's insane playacting, and our own exhaustion . . . why, we were a push-over!" Jean laughed shakily, snuggling against him. "Hypnosis?" she echoed obediently. "She believed so firmly, she made us believe? Naturally—" Her tone became brisk and matter-of-fact, if still a bit quavery— "there is no such thing as a . . . a . . . ." She broke off abruptly, pointing up at Miss Addie's gatepost, now more visible since the rain had slacked to a drizzle. "*Tom!*" she whispered. "*That sign of hers. . . .* Look at it! That's what she was talking about: that maybe it was what drew them here! . . . See what the wind and rain have done to those letters, the *u* and the *e* in *Guests* . . .?"

Her husband craned to see . . . and gave a yelp of mirth. Jean giggled. They were still laughing—gaily, intimately, somehow no longer afraid of being parted by a grim shadow called *Death*—as they drove on down the highway through the rain-swept night.

For, what the sign on the gatepost, on closer inspection, had seemed rakishly to advertise was:

FARADAY HOUSE
Miss Adelaide Faraday, Prop.
Overnight Ghosts